THE EYE OF HEAVEN

Can **you** save the victim of a web of mystery

Allen Sharp

Cambridge University Press

Cambridge

London   New York   New Rochelle

Melbourne   Sydney

Read
this
first

This book may be like no book that you have read before, because **you** decide the story. It is just like having an adventure in real life. What happens in the book happens to **you**. You decide what to do next and, like a real-life adventure, the end may not always be a happy one. That is up to **you**.

There are plenty of thrills and scares and you will have lots of chances to decide what you would do if you were really caught up in the adventure.

As a senior officer in the Special Branch of London's Metropolitan Police, you are in charge of two important security operations. One is a meeting of the heads of several foreign states. The other is a visit by a Middle Eastern prince. He is in London to reclaim a priceless jewel locked for many years in a disused government vault.

A lot of other things are going on. A naked body has been washed up on a quiet south-coast beach. A dangerous criminal has escaped from prison and is on the run. An old lady reports strange noises from the empty flat above her and sees

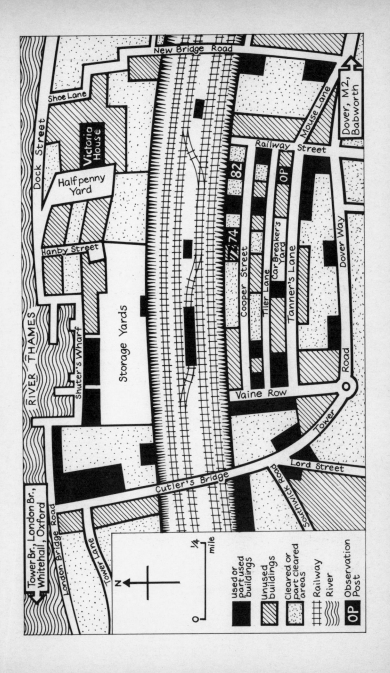

1

It was no doubt generous of Guthrie to insist on my sharing his Sunday lunch whenever we were both in Babworth. But it was not an occasion which I enjoyed.

He had just carved another slice from the usual joint of beef and added it to my plate, ignoring my protest that I already had sufficient. It was very underdone, as always, with the blood still oozing from it.

'Had an interesting post mortem yesterday,' he said, beginning to carve for himself. 'Thought when I was doing my report that it might be one for your lot.'

He always referred to my Section as 'your lot', mainly because he wasn't very sure what exactly 'my lot' did. I tried to keep it that way, but it never stopped Guthrie from making guesses.

I had bought my small cottage in Babworth Cove three years ago, imagining that it was the sort of quiet place where I could escape from my work, and where no-one would know me. I hadn't counted on the owner of the next cottage being a Home Office pathologist. Worse than that, with Guthrie's London connections, it hadn't been long before he'd discovered that I worked under Balfour in Section 6 of Special Branch.

I was trying to ignore the blood, which was now running under my vegetables, knowing that Guthrie was about to tell his latest 'entertaining' story about some corpse he'd been cutting up.

'You'll know about this one – "local", you might say.'

I had heard that a body had been washed up in the Cove on Friday morning.

'Male, white, age about thirty-five, good physical condition. Body was completely naked – a bit unusual. Large quantity of alcohol in the stomach. Death due to drowning. Probably unconscious before he entered the water. No abrasions. Help yourself to gravy.'

He paused, obviously awaiting my reactions.

'So,' I said, 'had too much to drink. Fell off a boat – maybe even went in for a swim.'

'Good!' Guthrie replied, through a mouthful of beef. 'Very good – but wrong!'

Turn to page 2.

2

'I did a check on the blood alcohol level – almost nothing. He'd had a bottle of whisky poured down his throat either by force, or when he was already unconscious. Needle marks on one arm. Could be recent innoculations. One of them could be something else. Have to wait for the blood analysis. Got enough meat?'

I nodded. I was half choking on what I already had.

'It was the teeth that were interesting. One hollowed out molar, empty, but designed for a cyanide pellet. And he had an implanted artificial tooth. New technique, just developed in Germany. No. Not accidental drowning. I'd say a murdered German Government Agent.'

There was raspberry crumble for sweet. Guthrie had finished his before asking me if I would be interested in knowing where the body might have come from. Though the lunch had left me feeling slightly sick, Guthrie knew that he had got me interested and that the answer to his question was going to be 'Yes'. I was grateful to learn that what

Guthrie had in mind was a walk up to the old coastguard station on Babworth Point to see Nick Casson. I needed some fresh air!

Casson had seen us coming and was waiting at the door of the station to greet us.

'When I sees who it were a-comin',' he said, 'I guesses what you might be a-comin' for. You wants to know if I got any ideas about that body what I finds on the beach. We'll be needin' the charts. I put the kettle on an' we can be havin' a look over a cuppa tea.'

It wasn't my day. Casson brewed the kind of tea that makes your tongue curl at the edges!

'I been doin' a bit o' figurin' already,' he told us. 'Main shippin' lanes is too far out from the coast. Could be a private boat, but if it were me lookin', I'd be thinkin' on one o' they Channel Ferries from Boulogne. Body been in the water four days . . .' Guthrie was nodding in agreement, 'so, say last Monday morning. Not the early hours. Tides would be wrong.' (3)

3

Casson had been coastguard at Babworth for fifteen years before the station had been closed and he'd retired. Born near the Cove, he'd fished and sailed the waters around the coast since he'd been a child. Certainly, no-one knew the currents, the winds and the tides better than he did. I was impressed that his estimate of the time the body had been in the water was the same as Guthrie's.

Guthrie could have stumbled upon something important. I tried to get Balfour in London at his Kensington home. I was told that he was golfing in Scotland for the weekend. His wife wasn't certain where – or that was what Balfour had told her to say!

At ten o'clock on Sunday night, I decided to start things moving. I rang my London office and asked for Miles Harper who I knew was on late duty. Peterson answered the telephone. Harper had just left to go to Cooper Street where we had set up a routine observation on a house. Something had gone wrong. He didn't know what. I gave him a list of enquiries I wanted making – the answers to be on my desk by Monday lunch time.

I'd said I would be back in the office late Monday morning. I got up at seven, went for a walk on the beach, and stopped on the way back to breakfast to pick up the morning papers in the High Street.

The body on the beach story had been in Saturday's Babworth Gazette. I hadn't expected it to get further, but there it was in one of the more sensational national dailies – 'Mystery of Naked Body in Secluded Cove'. That was a pity. The killer – if 'killer' there was – would now be alerted to possible investigations and would be that much more careful.

Something Casson had said flashed back into my mind – 'not the early hours of Monday morning'. How do you get rid of a naked body from a crowded ferry in broad daylight?

The Dover ferry terminals were only a twenty minute car journey from Babworth. I might get more answers on the spot than from my London office (5). But I might spend all day and still come up with nothing more than Peterson. I was also curious to know what had 'gone wrong' in Cooper Street (7).

4

Since I'd left the car, one of the dockside cranes had begun to unload large crates from the hold of an Algerian freighter. They were being stacked along the water side of the wharf. I got into the car and had started to move off when someone shouted a warning.

There was nothing in front of me. I looked up. Hanging some twenty feet above the car, swinging on the end of the crane's jib, was one of the large packing cases. It seemed to have part slipped out of its rope cradle.

As I stared upward, I saw the wire holding the crate slacken for a split second and then pull taught. The crate was sliding in the cradle! I banged my gears into reverse – but it was too late. The crate smashed down on the front of the car, shattering the windscreen and scattering its load of metal castings all around me. I tried the doors of the car, but the weight of the castings lying against them was holding them shut. I grabbed my coat, wrapped it around my forearm and smashed out most of the rest of the glass from the windscreen. As I crawled out onto the bonnet, I could smell petrol leaking from the engine which was still running. I flung myself to the ground, rolling among the castings, picked myself up and was running again before the car exploded behind me. I glanced back at the flames before I ran on – heading for the crane.

I couldn't see into the crane's cab from the ground. I started to mount the steel ladders. I was half way up when I heard the sound of a car engine revving up. I looked down. A white Mercedes was emerging from the open doors of one of the storage sheds. It did a tight turn and roared off down the wharf – too far off and too fast to catch its registration.

The real crane driver was still in his cab with a bruise of the back of his head that was coming up like a hen's egg.

Two thoughts were passing through my own head. Had I any chance of having that white Mercedes stopped before it got out of the dock area (6), or should I be aiming to find out how someone knew who I was and why they had just made the attempt to kill me (8)?

5

When I got to Dover, I started with the nearest of the ferries, the car ferry office near the Eastern Dock. As I expected, Peterson had been making enquiries before me – mainly about any 'missing' passengers. Again, as I expected, none had been reported.

One thing, I hadn't expected. If Guthrie's and Casson's estimates of when and where the body had entered the water were anywhere near correct, then there was only one ferry it could have come from.

There had been dense fog in the Channel all through the early hours of Monday morning. The first ferry to sail was at eight o'clock from Boulogne. It had run into fog again well before reaching Dover – and there were no more ferry sailings in either direction until well after noon. The fog answered my question about how you threw a body overboard in broad daylight, without someone seeing you.

The ferry which had sailed was owned by the D and B Line in whose offices I was standing. Lois Shepherd, the office manager, had been as helpful as she could be. The problem was that none of that ferry's crew was available at just that moment.

'Wait!' said Mrs Shepherd, getting up from her desk. 'That looks like George Colby just come in.'

I saw through the half glass partition that someone had entered the outer office. Colby was brought in and introduced as the chief steward who was aboard the Monday morning ferry. I told him what I wanted to know: anything unusual – no matter how trivial. He shook his head.

'Nothing,' he said. 'Fog makes the passengers that bit nervous. You wouldn't get a quieter crossing.'

I caught a quick flicker of a smile cross his face.

'Tell me, anyway!' I said.

'Couldn't be anything you're looking for. It was after we'd docked and I was doing the usual rounds of the cabins. I picked up a newspaper. Somebody'd been marking up the racing page – just one horse. I has the occasional flutter, so I puts a pound on it. Came up at fifty to one!'

It wasn't what I was looking for! The rest of the crew wouldn't be in until next day, so I decided to get straight back to London. My car was behind the Customs Shed on the cargo wharf of the dock (4).

6

The crane driver had half 'come to'. He had no idea what had hit him. I knew that some of these newer cranes had a few of the luxuries of modern technology – like a radio telephone – so I asked him.

'Yes,' he said, still nursing his head. 'On the right. Who do you want to speak to?'

I asked if there was a line to the dock office. He nodded – immediately regretting that movement of his head!

'Yes,' he added, 'Channel four.'

I got through to the office. They'd seen the explosion from the office window, which made it easier to persuade them to do what I wanted without some kind of argument. I told them to contact the dock police. If a white Mercedes had still not left the dock area, to stop it – for any reason they liked to think up. We also needed an ambulance and a relief crane driver.

I stayed with the crane driver. The ambulance was no more than a couple of minutes in coming. The message back from the dock police took longer. There were five gates to check.

The white Mercedes had passed through Gate 4

all of five minutes ago. The car carried CD plates and the driver's papers gave him diplomatic immunity. The man on the gate couldn't remember either the driver's name or nationality. There'd been a lot of traffic coming through the gate at the time. All that he could remember was that the man driving the car looked like an Arab.

I went back to the car ferry offices. Word of my 'accident' had already got around. No-one had left the office after I had. No-one had been in asking questions about me. Mrs Shepherd was only too pleased to let me wait in the offices until I got someone to bring me another car down from London.

I left the message that whoever brought the car should be prepared for a one or two night stay in Dover, possibly a trip to Boulogne. I wanted every member of the Monday morning ferry crew interviewed.

There was now no doubt in my mind about Guthrie's theory of a killing. What was worrying me when I did start my trip back to London was whether I was meant to be the next victim (**10**)!

7

Cooper Street was more or less on the way back to my office. On the south side of the Thames, it was in an area east of Tower Bridge. Most of its buildings were early Victorian, and it was in the process of demolition and redevelopment.

It looked like parts of London after the wartime bombing – blocks of two or three houses with gaps between them. Some of the gaps were still filled with rubble. Others had been cleared and one or two were being used for temporary businesses, like builder's stores or car breaker's yards. Of the houses which still stood, some were occupied, or part occupied, despite efforts by the local council to persuade their occupiers to move. It was one such house, 82 Cooper Street, which was under observation.

The spot chosen for the observation was an empty house with its back entrance in the next street, Tiler Lane. I'd parked the car at the end of Tiler Lane and was walking towards the house when a sizeable stone struck the ground in front of me. It hit it with such force that it bounced up again, chipping some mortar from an already crumbling brick wall past which I was walking.

I looked in the direction from which the stone had come. Across one of the open sites, I was looking at a house in Cooper Street. Seated at an open first floor window was an old woman. She was busy reloading a large and particularly deadly looking catapult! I didn't wait for her to take aim. I scrambled over the wall, landing on the other side amongst a heap of rusting scrap metal. I was immediately struck on the head by something soft, but heavy, which disappeared into the heap of metal below me.

I untangled myself sufficiently from the metal to look for what had hit me. Clearly visible, but out of my reach, was a cat. From the way it was lying and the blood on its head, it was certainly dead. The sight gave me a sickening feeling. The cat had obviously got the stone that was meant for me. The old woman had to be crazy!

Keeping my head down, I clambered down from the heap of metal into what I could see was a car breaker's yard. I was covered in a mixture of rust, oil and dirt, not to mention a smear of blood from the dead cat (**9**).

8

I saw that the cab of the crane was fitted with a radio telephone. The crane driver had half 'come to' and was able to tell me that if I switched the telephone to Channel 4, I could speak to the dock office. They had seen the explosion from the office window – which meant that I wasn't going to have to do a lot of explaining. I told them to get an ambulance for the crane driver and I would stay with him until its arrival.

The ambulance was not long in coming. I left it to the ambulance crew to get the driver down while I went back to the car ferry offices. Word of my 'accident' had got there ahead of me. I used Lois Shepherd's office to ring London and get someone to bring me another car. I warned them that whoever brought it should be prepared for a one or two night stay in Dover. I wanted every member of that Monday morning ferry to be interviewed.

Meanwhile, I turned my attention back to trying to discover how the 'accident' could have been arranged so quickly when I hadn't even decided to visit Dover until that morning.

I didn't get any answers. No-one had left the ferry office after me. No-one had been in asking questions about me. I noticed Colby was missing. Shepherd said he was in the locker room, downstairs.

Colby hadn't been expecting a visitor. He shut his locker door quickly, but not before I'd caught a glimpse of several bottles of spirits. His face was the colour of beetroot. I suggested he might want to tell me something.

It was nothing very sinister. The bottles were his unofficial 'perks' which forgetful passengers occasionally left in their cabins. I was only interested in Monday morning.

'Nothing,' he told me. 'There was only one bottle – and that was empty. It was in the cabin where I found the racing tip – so I can't really grumble.'

'Empty bottle of what?' I asked.

'Pretty sure it was whisky,' was the reply.

My car arrived an hour later and I decided to pay my visit to Cooper Street (**10**).

9

There were only two ways out of the yard. One was to climb over the gates into the next street, Tanner's Lane. The other was to get back over the wall. There were often people in Tanner's Lane and I didn't want to be seen climbing over the gates. Tiler Lane, being a back street, was usually quiet but, to keep out of range of the old woman and her catapult, I'd have to scramble over the wall at the far corner where there was an even larger heap of old scrap.

I settled for getting out over the scrap. I now had to walk back to where I'd left my car, then walk down Tanner's Lane to reach the front door of the observation post. My clothes were in a mess before I got out of the yard, and the scramble to get back over the wall had not improved them! When I reached my car, I decided to get in and see if I could do anything to tidy myself up. It also seemed like a good opportunity to call my office and tell them where I was.

Peterson had left a message for me. He'd sent off the photograph and fingerprints of the body to Interpol and was awaiting a reply. There were no reports of 'missing' passengers, but he had discovered one thing which could narrow down enquiries. Because of fog, only one ferry, the eight o'clock car ferry from Boulogne, had sailed between midnight on Sunday and noon on Monday. Fog might also be the answer to how a passenger could 'disappear' in broad daylight!

Peterson was now in Dover but had, so far, only talked to the ferry's chief steward. The steward remembered nothing unusual – though he had good reason to remember the trip. On checking the cabins after docking at Dover, he'd found a newspaper, open at the racing page, and with one horse marked. He'd put a pound on it and it had come up at fifty to one that afternoon at the Doncaster Races. Unfortunately, it didn't help solve a possible murder! Peterson would be back when he'd seen the rest of the crew.

My efforts to improve my appearance had not been successful. I still looked like a scarecrow. Should I still go to the observation post – where they'd get a good laugh at how I came to be in this state (**14**), or should I make it wait until I'd been back to the office to change my clothes (**12**)?

10

Cooper Street was on the way to my office, on the south side of the Thames, east of Tower Bridge. Mainly early Victorian houses, it was an area in the process of demolition and redevelopment. It looked like parts of London after the wartime bombing – blocks of two or three houses with gaps between them. Some of the gaps were still filled with rubble. Some had been cleared and a few were being used for temporary businesses like builder's stores and car breaker's yards. Despite the efforts of the local council to clear them, some of the houses were still occupied. It was one such house at 82 Cooper Street which was under observation.

The spot chosen for the observation was an empty house with its back entrance in the next street, Tiler Lane. I parked the car in Tanner's Lane. On my way to the observation post I had to walk past a fenced-off site filled with scrap cars. Two children, a small boy and a slightly older girl, were climbing over the gates as I passed. The girl almost jumped down onto my head. She looked at me sheepishly.

'Our Sammy's stuck!' she said.

'Stuck where?' I asked.

'In there,' was the reply. 'We was playin' among the cars an' 'e slips. Now, 'e's stuck!'

I helped the girl back over the gates and climbed after her. Sammy was indeed 'stuck' – in a pile of rusty scrap metal at the back of the yard against a brick wall. It was his foot that was caught and I had to pull away quite a bit of metal before we could release it. Sammy's first words as I pulled him out were not of thanks.

'There's a dead cat in there. It's been shot.'

He pointed down amongst the metal. I could see the cat. I couldn't reach it. From where it was and the way it was lying, it looked as if it had come off the wall above. There was a lot of blood on its head. I couldn't believe it had been shot – a stone, maybe.

I got the boy and girl out of the yard and the three children went off happily. I wasn't so happy. My clothes were covered in rust, oil and dirt. Should I go on to the post (**14**), or first return to the office to get myself cleaned up (**12**)?

11

I'd arranged for Harper to meet me at Halfpenny Yard, outside Victoria House. The Yard was not, in fact, a stone's throw from Cooper Street, but separated from it by the railway which made it some distance off by road.

Like the rest of the area, the Yard had not escaped the work of the demolition men. Victoria House itself should have come down long ago. It had been declared unsafe and its Government Offices emptied all of twenty years before. It remained standing only because of the large security vaults beneath it. These housed huge quantities of official documents which remained there for want of suitable alternative storage.

Very recently we had discovered that they also contained something more surprising. In 1932, the Sultanate of Bohara, one of the small Gulf States, was taken over by a revolutionary government. The then young Sultan had fled to England, bringing with him the most precious item of the Boharan 'crown jewels' – a single perfect sapphire weighing 203 carats and known as the 'Eye of Heaven'. Why the stone, still in its sealed package, should have been placed in Victoria House, was something of a mystery. What now mattered was that power in Bohara had been restored to the joint rulership of the Sultan's two sons, the Princes Hassan and Ali. In two days' time, Prince Ali would visit Victoria House to reclaim the Eye of Heaven. Because of the doubts about the safety of the building, efforts had been made to persuade the Boharan Ambassador to agree to the handing-over ceremony taking place elsewhere. It was no use. The Princes felt that it should take place in the vaults as a mark of respect to their late father, the Sultan. My job was to protect both the Prince and the stone. We couldn't afford to let anything spoil our present friendly relations with Bohara.

In case of some emergency, I wanted Harper to know the security arrangements as well as I did. We'd been through transport, positioning of armed police, and the search of those entering the vault. I wanted Harper to see the vaults themselves.

Some time in the twenties, they had been fitted with a new 'safe type' door, with what must have been one of the earliest time locks (**15**).

12

When I got to the office, Harper was there, having returned from Cooper Street just before me. He explained what the 'trouble' was.

The place we'd chosen for observing 82 Cooper Street should have been ideal. An empty house in Tanner's Lane, it backed onto Tiler Lane and overlooked 82 across a part-demolished building. From it we could watch any comings and goings with little chance of being seen ourselves.

82 was occupied by the mother, wife and family of Paddy Roper. Roper had got twelve years for the London Wall bullion job. A million in silver was still missing. Fourteen days ago, Roper had escaped from Oakhurst Prison. He'd been there for eight years, during which time his family had lived at 82. It wasn't exactly the best part of London, but Roper had somehow looked after them while he'd been 'inside'. They weren't short of money. There was a slim chance that he would try to see them.

The missing million worried us less than Roper. He'd almost killed a security guard on the bullion job and had injured two warders while he'd been in Oakhurst. He had to be caught.

The 'trouble' was neither Roper, nor his family at 82. The trouble lived at 74 Cooper Street. It was an old woman who occupied the first floor flat – an old woman with several peculiarities.

She never appeared to sleep. She had a voice like a foghorn, was a crack shot with a catapult, and assumed that every stranger she saw was some part of the council's 'plot' to get her out of the house. She'd even identified our observation post and had reported us to the police!

'If somebody doesn't do something about her,' Harper said, 'we may as well pack it in.'

I already had one job fixed for the morning. A Middle Eastern prince was visiting a government vault in Halfpenny Yard and I still had some checking to do on the security arrangements. I could see that I now had two jobs.

I only had to decide which to visit first – the occupant of number 74 Cooper Street (**13**), or the vault in Halfpenny Yard (**11**).

13

Number 74 Cooper Street had neither door knocker, nor bell. I banged on the wood panels. A head stuck itself out from the first floor window.

'If you're the Council, I'm out,' she called down.

'I'm from the police,' I called back. 'I understand you've been making a complaint.'

'You don't look like police.'

'I'm in the plain clothes branch.'

'You'd better come up. Door's not locked.'

Mrs McGee's 'front room' was much tidier than I expected. I noticed a catapult and a heap of stones on a table by the open window. Through it, I could see across to the scrap yard in Tanner's Lane. She saw me looking at the catapult.

'Trouble with cats?' I asked her.

'Cats? Wouldn't catch me harming a cat. I like cats. It's certain people I can't abide – specially people from the Council.'

'You'd better tell me about it,' I said.

'Not much to tell. They want this house. I tell them they're welcome to it when I'm dead and gone – but they think that might take too long. So now they're trying to frighten me out. They'll find that I don't frighten that easy!'

I asked how they were trying to frighten her. She told me about 'suspicious' people she'd seen going up and down Tiler Lane at night as well as through the day. Something 'funny' was going on in a house in Tanner's Lane. I knew very well what that was about. Then she surprised me.

'Now they've started creepin' about upstairs – and there's them funny lights.'

I'd gathered that the flats above and below were empty. A quick trip up the one staircase revealed that the door of the flat above was securely boarded up. Mrs McGee admitted that the noises might be from the empty house next door. I asked her about the 'lights'.

'Only seen them once – last night, out of the bedroom at the back. They was like little red spots dancin' about on the buildings. Maybe they think as I'll think it's the Martians,' she cackled, 'but I know it's them upstairs!' (**17**)

14

When I got to the post, I found that I had just missed Harper who had returned to the office. Parks and Williams were on watch. It was Parks who put me in the picture. The story would have been laughable if it hadn't presented us with a serious problem.

The place we'd chosen for the observation should have been ideal. It was an empty house in Tanner's Lane. It backed onto Tiler Lane and overlooked 82 Cooper Street across a part-demolished building. From it we could see the comings and goings at 82 with very little chance of being seen ourselves.

The house we were watching was occupied by the mother, wife and children of Paddy Roper. Roper had been sent down for twelve years for the London Wall bullion job. A million in silver was still missing. Fourteen days ago, Roper had escaped from Oakhurst Prison. Roper had been 'inside' for eight years, during which time his family had lived in Cooper Street. It wasn't the best part of London, but they weren't short of money. Roper had somehow looked after them and there was a slim chance that he would try to see them.

The missing million worried us less than the fact that Roper was dangerous. He'd almost killed a guard on the bullion job and had twice injured prison warders. He had to be caught.

The 'problem' was not either Roper or his family at 82. The problem lived at 74 Cooper Street. The first floor of 74 was occupied by an eighty-three year old woman with several peculiarities. She never appeared to sleep. She had a voice like a foghorn, was a crack shot with a catapult, and believed that every stranger she saw was part of the local council 'plot' to get her out of the house. She'd already identified our observation post and reported us to the police!

There was nowhere else we could move to. Somebody had to convince the old woman that we were nothing to do with the council. I knew who was going to have to do it but, with the state of my clothes, now was not the best time.

I already had one job lined up for the morning – checking on security for the visit of a Middle Eastern prince to a government vault in Halfpenny Yard. Which should I visit first – number 74 (**13**), or the vault (**11**)?

15

Selby and Mayhew, the original installers of the safe door and time lock, had already been back to check the mechanism. Having established that the package containing the jewel was in its proper place, the safe had been shut and the time lock set for 10.00 a.m. on Thursday morning. That was the time for the ceremony and there was no way the door could be opened until then.

All Harper was able to see was the small ante-room in the basement, outside the locked door.

'It looks quite a museum piece,' he said.

I had to agree, though I did point out that it was a compliment to the workmanship that it worked as reliably as ever. Nothing had had to be replaced except the light over the door which came on when the time lock released. The original red light had burned out and was of a pattern no longer made. We'd had to make do with a white one.

Once outside in the street again, I reminded Harper of what I saw as the point of maximum risk. The car carrying the Prince would stop outside the building. He then had a four-yard walk to the door.

'If I were planning to assassinate him,' I told

Harper, 'I would do it in those four yards.'

Harper appreciated my worry. With empty and half-demolished buildings around, it was going to be very difficult to search them well enough to be absolutely certain that they weren't hiding a gunman.

'What's beyond there?' Harper asked, looking at the end of the Yard.

It was just a front wall of one of the part-demolished buildings, the windows now only empty holes in the stonework.

'The railway,' I answered, 'and on the other side of the railway, is Cooper Street.

We'd spent longer in the Yard than I had intended. Balfour was expecting me to report to him in his Whitehall Office that arrangements for the Prince's visit were complete and to my satisfaction (**18**). For some reason, the reminder that Cooper Street was just across the railway from the Yard, had raised a doubt in my mind. It was a doubt I couldn't quite put my finger on. I could make Balfour wait until I'd seen the old lady at number 74 (**16**).

16

I called at my office on my way to Cooper Street to collect a good pair of binoculars. A message had arrived from the German police. They'd identified the body on Babworth beach as that of Klaus Weiler, a German Government Agent. We also had the pathologist's report confirming almost no alcohol in the blood, but a large quantity of a barbiturate. Guthrie had been right. It was murder.

On Thursday evening, a meeting of European heads of state was beginning at Cherton Castle in Worcestershire. Weiler, like other foreign agents, had been on his way there to discuss security arrangements. It didn't seem to be a good enough reason for murder.

Cherton had been my responsibility but, at the last minute, Balfour had decided to take charge himself. So it was Balfour's worry. It obviously had no connection with the Prince's visit to the Halfpenny Yard vault.

I stopped my car outside 74 Cooper Street. A first-floor window shot open and a head poked out. I knew I was looking at Mrs McGee.

'If you're from the Council,' she called out, 'then you can get back in your motor – because I'm not letting you in here.'

'I'm from the police,' I said.

'You don't look like police, and that's not a police car.'

I explained that I was the 'plain clothes' branch and that I'd come about her complaint. Eventually she let me in.

Her room was neater than expected, though I did notice the catapult and the heap of stones on a table by the front window – a window that over-looked the car breaker's yard in Tanner's Lane.

'Trouble with cats?' I asked.

'No. Cats don't bother me. I likes cats. It's certain people I can't abide – like them from the Council.'

I asked her to tell me about it.

'Not much to tell,' she replied. 'They want me out and I won't go. They've tried everything else, so now they think that they can frighten me out!'

(**22**)

17

The old woman might have been eccentric, but there seemed no reason to think that she hadn't got all her wits about her. I believed what she'd told me. I knew what could be seen from the front of the house. I asked if I might see out of the back windows. After my assurance that I wouldn't look at the unmade bed, she took me into her bedroom.

The window looked directly across the railway. At the other side of the tracks were several part-demolished buildings. Some still had walls standing, so that apart from the gaps in the walls formed by what had been windows, it was difficult to see what lay beyond.

'Do you know that side of the railway well?' I asked her.

'Should do. Lived here eighty-three years. Used to play on the railway when I was a bit younger.'

'What's beyond the wall right opposite – between the two buildings that still have roofs on them?'

She thought.

'Hanby Street – no, 'cause that's the old boot and shoe factory. That's the end of Halfpenny Yard.'

I told Mrs McGee that I'd look into her complaints, though it might take a few days. That way, I'd bought some time for our observation post. But I wasn't only intending to keep the old lady quiet. She'd now got me interested in cats, funny lights – and Halfpenny Yard!

There was an old government building in Halfpenny Yard – Victoria House, long since declared unsafe, but still kept for the sake of its large basement vaults which housed huge quantities of old government records. It also contained something unusual.

In 1932, the deposed Sultan of the Middle Eastern State of Bohara, had fled to England, carrying a 'royal' jewel – a perfect 203 carat sapphire, the 'Eye of Heaven'. It still lay in a sealed package in the Victoria House vault. Power in Bohara had recently been restored to the joint rulership of the Sultan's two sons, Hassan and Ali. On Thursday Prince Ali was to visit the vault to reclaim the Eye of Heaven.

Mrs McGee had already delayed my visit to Halfpenny Yard. I decided to delay it for a few minutes more (**20**).

18

Balfour was worried – worried enough not to be too interested in the visit of Prince Ali. We'd got news about the body on the beach at Babworth. The German police had identified it as that of Klaus Weiler, a German Government Agent. We also had the pathologist's report. Blood tests confirmed almost no alcohol, but a large quantity of a barbiturate. Guthrie's theory was right. It was murder.

On Thursday evening, a meeting of European heads of state was beginning at Cherton Castle in Worcestershire. Weiler, like other foreign agents, had been on his way to Cherton to discuss security arrangements. It didn't seem to be a good enough reason for his murder. Balfour agreed, but still wasn't too happy. He'd decided, at the last minute, to relieve me of the Cherton operation and take over himself. I was grateful. The murder could have no connection with the Prince's visit – and Balfour now had more to think about than keeping me talking in his office.

With some time now in hand, I collected a good pair of binoculars from my office and went straight on to Cooper Street. The first response I got to my knocking on the door of number 74, was the sound of a window being opened above me. The woman whose name I now knew as Mrs McGee was leaning out of the window. She had a large flower pot in her hands.

'If you're from the Council,' she called down, 'all you'll get from me is this pot on your head!'

'I'm from the police,' I called back.

'Don't look like police. Sure you're not Council?'

I convinced her that I was police and had come about her complaint. I was invited upstairs.

The flat was neater than I expected, though I couldn't help noticing the large catapult and the heap of stones on the table by the window – a window which overlooked the car breaker's yard in Tanner's Lane.

'Trouble with cats?' I asked.

'Cats? I like cats. It's certain people I can't abide – specially that lot from the Council.'

I suggested she tell me about it.

'It's simple,' she replied. 'They want me out of this house. They've tried everything else, now they're trying to frighten me out!' **(22)**

19

I took a chance and shone my light inside. It picked out a long corridor, which was empty. I ventured inside. I had gone only a few paces before I heard voices – two voices, both raised in anger. One of them, I recognised as the Cockney tones of Paddy Roper. The other had a foreign accent. They were coming from the direction of the staircase down to the vaults.

Suddenly, there was a shot, then a second, which merged with an ear-splitting explosion. The whole building shook and smoke was already billowing up the staircase from the vaults. There was no going down there! I ran out of the building to the nearest phone box, to ring fire, ambulance and police.

In the small anteroom outside the vaults, two bodies were recovered. One was Roper. The other has never been identified. There had certainly been an explosion, though its exact source could not be pinpointed. The safe door to the vaults was damaged and jammed, but the contents of the vaults seemed to be unharmed.

The Prince's visit had to be postponed and he and his party returned to Bohara the next day. A month later, Prince Ali was killed in Bohara in a car accident. Six months later, Balfour was approached by the Boharan Ambassador, requesting that the Eye of Heaven be handed to him in its original package, when it would be returned to Bohara by special messenger. The ceremonial handing-over was no longer felt appropriate.

There were one or two loose ends surrounding the affair that were never settled to my satisfaction.

Though it may have had no connection with anything in which I had been involved, Guthrie discovered the body of Nick Casson in the old coast guard station at Babworth Point on the same night I had been chasing Roper. Casson had been shot. There was no apparent motive. The cat on which I had been awaiting an answer, unaccountably 'disappeared' from the pathology laboratory.

I have always felt certain that Balfour either knew or guessed something which he wasn't telling me – something to do with the Eye of Heaven. All he said when I asked him was, 'As Nelson discovered, it's sometimes useful to have a "blind eye".'

20

I put the car out of sight and walked to the
observation post. Harper had left me a message,
thinking I might call there and knowing I would
want the news as soon as possible. The German
police had identified the body on the beach as that
of Klaus Weiler, a German Government Agent.
The Pathology report had also confirmed Guthrie's
theory. There was almost no alcohol in the blood,
but a large quantity of a barbiturate. It was murder.

On Thursday evening, a meeting of heads of
state of European countries was beginning at
Cherton Castle in Worcestershire. Weiler, like
other foreign agents, had been on his way to
Cherton to discuss security. That would have
been my job if Balfour hadn't made a last minute
decision to supervise the operation himself. I was
grateful. The murder had no obvious connection
with the Prince's visit to Halfpenny Yard on
Thursday morning.

I phoned the office and told Harper to meet me
at Halfpenny Yard in half an hour, and to bring
with a him a good pair of binoculars.

I told the two men on watch at the observation

post that I'd been to see Mrs McGee. There should be no more trouble, at least for the next few days, but they should start using Tanner's Lane instead of Tiler Lane. That way, Mrs McGee was less likely to see them.

That wasn't the main reason for my visit to the post. I wanted a dirty and unpleasant job done and I preferred to ask the favour myself. The two on duty would be relieved in about an hour's time.

I wanted them to go to the car breaker's yard in Tanner's Lane and to get the dead cat out from the heap of scrap metal. I wanted it to be removed carefully and then taken to the pathology laboratory. What I wanted to know, and quickly, was exactly how the cat had met its untimely death.

My staff didn't usually question my instructions. I wouldn't have blamed them if they'd wanted a reason for the job I'd just asked them to do. The only truthful answer I could have given was that I was 'playing a hunch'. But they hadn't asked, and I thought I should get on to Halfpenny Yard before they did (**21**).

21

Victoria House was one of the few buildings left standing in Halfpenny Yard and certainly the only one still used. I knew Harper would be some minutes in arriving and decided to take another look at the vault in the basement.

There was not a lot to see, mainly because for the moment it was not possible to get further than the anteroom outside the vault door. Fitted some time in the twenties, it must have been one of the earliest 'safe type' doors to have a time-lock mechanism. It had very recently been overhauled and, despite its age, nothing had needed replacement except the light over the door which came on when the lock was released. The original red light had burned out and, being an obsolete fitting, only a white bulb could be found to replace it.

The package containing the 'Eye of Heaven' had been checked as being in its place, the door had been shut and the time lock set for 10.00 a.m. on Thursday morning. That was the time for the ceremony and there was no way the door could be opened until then.

Harper arrived with the binoculars. I'd had one

worry about security. The Prince would arrive by car and then had a four-yard walk to the building. It was going to be hard to search the half-demolished buildings around. If I'd wanted to assassinate the Prince, I'd have done it in those four yards.

I took the binoculars and directed them at the part-demolished building at the end of the Yard. I wanted to know what could be seen through the holes which had once been windows. It was through the fourth hole that I tried that I was able to focus up on something I recognised – the pink curtains with red tulips at Mrs McGee's bedroom window. I had only to bend my knees slightly, and I was looking at the window of the empty flat above. I was standing exactly where Prince Ali would be walking on Thursday.

I had nothing but the word of an eccentric old woman and a dead cat to go on – that and a 'gut' feeling. I could wait to hear how the cat died (**25**), or I could wait until dark to do a little illegal breaking and entering into the top floor of number 74 Cooper Street (**23**).

22

I was told first about the 'suspicious' people who she'd seen 'creeping' up and down Tiler Lane – at all hours of the night, as well as through the day. She thought there was something going on at one of the houses down there. I knew very well what all that was about, but the next thing she said surprised me.

'Now, they've started creepin' about upstairs – and there's the funny lights.'

I'd gathered that the flats above and below her were empty. A quick trip up the one staircase in the house, revealed that the door of the flat above was securely boarded up. Mrs McGee admitted that the noises might have come from the empty house next door. I asked about the 'funny' lights.

'Only seen them once,' she said, 'last night, out of the bedroom at the back. It was like little red spots dancing about on the buildings. Maybe they think that I'll be thinking that it's the Martians,' she cackled, 'but I'm not stupid. I knows it's them upstairs.'

I asked if I might see the view from her bedroom window at the back of the house. It looked over the railway, and beyond that were some half-demolished buildings. I asked her if she knew where Halfpenny Yard was. She pointed it out.

I focused the binoculars onto what had been the window spaces of the building which hid the Yard from view. I suddenly realised I was looking at something I recognised – the doorway to Victoria House.

I told Mrs McGee that I would look carefully into her complaints, though it might take a few days. I hoped that would buy some time for the people in the observation post, but it wasn't an idle promise. Mrs McGee had raised a few questions in my mind.

I went back to the observation post and told the two on duty that when they were relieved, I wanted them to go to the car breaker's yard and find me one dead cat. The body was to go to Pathology for a quick answer on how the cat had died. I was wondering whether to do a bit of illegal breaking and entering into the empty house next to 74, that night (23), or wait for the answer about the cat (25).

23

At a little after midnight, I forced open a downstair window at the back of number 72 Cooper Street and climbed into the empty house. Shielding my torch so that the light wouldn't be seen from outside, I made my way quietly up the stairs.

I could have applied for a search warrant and made my visit official, but I had so little in the way of hard 'evidence', I was reluctant to make a fool of myself.

I had only one fact. Halfpenny Yard was visible from Cooper Street. More important, it was the bit of Halfpenny Yard which the Prince would have to cross on Thursday morning. I'd checked the distance and it was just under a thousand yards. In theory, a marksman with a high-powered rifle fitted with a laser sight, could hit a target at that distance.

What had stuck in my mind was Mrs McGee's 'funny lights'. The 'give away' of a rifle with a laser sight is the bright red dot of light used to find its target. I was guessing that such a rifle might have been used on the cat as 'target practice'. That would be all the confirmation I needed – but I knew that Pathology could be very slow in coming up with answers. Time was one thing I hadn't got.

The catches on the windows at the back and front of both the first and top floors were rusty and hadn't been moved for a long time. That told me two things. No marksman had been using 72. As for 74, there were only two ways into the top floor. One was by a door which was well boarded up. The other could have been across the roof – except that that would have meant using the windows, and the windows in 72 hadn't been opened. I was about to leave when I heard a noise – next door, in the top flat of 74!

I was standing beside a cupboard set into the wall which divided 72 and 74. Some of these had once been bigger houses, later divided into two. I opened the cupboard door. The back wall was just lathe and plaster and part of it had been smashed away. I was looking through it at the back of another door – of a similar cupboard in number 74.

I put out my torch, climbed through and opened the other door. Whatever hit me, threw me half senseless to the floor (**24**).

24

Trying to stagger back to my feet, my head still swimming from the blow, I was conscious of the sound of running feet – back through the room which I had just left in number 72. Unsteadily, I followed.

I reached the door of the next room to hear the footsteps now taking the stairs two at a time. My torch was still in my hand. I shone it down the stair well. From one of the half-landings below me came a flash of light and the whine of a bullet which splintered the handrail near where I was clinging to it. In those brief seconds, I had seen a face – the face of Paddy Roper!

I put out the torch and stumbled down the stairs in the dark. The footsteps were now on the ground floor. They hesitated. Roper was going out through the window I had used to come in.

I reached the window in time to see Roper sitting astride the backyard wall. On the other side of it lay the railway. He heard, or saw me. He raised his pistol to take a second shot. Above me, a window shot open. I saw Roper look up. He gave a sharp cry as the gun spun out of his hand. There was a louder cry as I saw him put his hand up to the side of his head and drop out of sight over the wall.

I jumped from the window, calling up into the darkness, 'Police, Mrs McGee! Don't fire! Leave the rest to me. Thanks for the help!'

She shouted something back, but it was lost as I swung myself over the wall where Roper had vanished. He was not there. Before me, the railway was dappled with light. I'd lost him!

I decided on taking a chance. The best way out at the other side was probably Halfpenny Yard. I hoped Roper knew the same thing. I made straight across the tracks, scrambling over the broken wall of the building at the back of the Yard. Now it was tricky. There was practically no light. I had to feel my way forward, not knowing whether Roper was waiting there, or whether he still had the gun.

I was out of the half-demolished building and into the Yard. There was still one street lamp. The Yard was empty, but the light showed up the doorway of Victoria House. The door was open (**19**)!

25

On Wednesday morning, I found a polite little note on my office desk. It was from Parks and Williams, the two officers who had had the job of recovering the dead cat. It said, 'Wish to report cat has been recovered and delivered to Pathology as instructed. Assume you will authorise expenses for cleaning and replacement of clothing dirtied or damaged in recovery operation.'

They would get their expenses. Whether I made it official, or paid them out of my own pocket, depended upon the answer I got on the cat.

I had only one hard fact to go on until then. 74 Cooper Street had a clear view of one small area of Halfpenny Yard – an area across which Prince Ali would have to walk tomorrow morning as he entered Victoria House. I'd checked the distance on a map. It was just under a thousand yards. I'd asked our arms expert, 'Is it possible to hit a target with any accuracy at that range?' The answer I'd got was, 'Possibly – given a special enough rifle fitted with a laser sight.'

The 'give away' of a rifle fitted with a laser sight

is the small, bright red spot of light which it uses to mark its target. Mrs McGee had spoken of someone upstairs and moving spots of red light 'dancing about' the buildings. The cat I had seen in the car breaker's yard did look as if it had been shot in the head. It still could have been a stone from Mrs McGee's catapult – though she would deny it. If Pathology showed that the cat had been used as target practice for a high powered rifle, I would have something to go on other than what might be the imagination of an eccentric old lady.

By mid afternoon, I had had no answer from Pathology. I phoned them. They had a lot of work on hand, 'all of it, urgent'. They would do their best for me. But time was running out.

I tried Guthrie at his Babworth cottage. He was home and, 'Yes', if I brought the cat, he would do a post mortem on it, on the spot.

I didn't like the idea of leaving London with the Prince's visit only hours away. Should I go to Babworth (**30**), or chance getting my answer in time from Pathology (**26**)?

26

I spent the evening in my flat and went to bed early. It didn't stop me from sleeping in on Thursday morning! I phoned Peterson, who lived not far away from me, to say that there were some papers to collect from my office and deliver to Balfour in Whitehall, before he left for Cherton. I also asked if there had been any answer about the cat. I was told, 'No'. It was too late to worry.

Peterson then announced that he was having trouble with his car and there would be few taxis about at that time of morning. I told him to walk round, collect my keys, and take my car. I'd use a taxi.

It was eight o'clock when I got to Whitehall. I'd also arranged to meet Harper there so that we could all go round together to the Royal Knightsbridge Hotel to pick up the Prince and his party at 9.30.

Balfour had left for Cherton, minutes before my arrival. Harper was there. So was Peterson – trying to stop the blood which was running from a long cut in his forehead by dabbing it with newspaper.

'Your car is wrapped around a lamp post in St

Martin's Lane,' he said. 'Someone had done a very expert job on loosening the fluid pipes to your brakes. Luckily I was moving very slowly in traffic when I tried to use them. I've sent for another car for you.'

'Are you all right?' I asked.

'Fine,' he answered, tearing himself off another piece of newspaper. I couldn't help noticing that what he was tearing up was the racing page.

'You went down to Dover for us, didn't you?' I said. 'I know the story about the 50–1 winner. It's never crossed my mind to ask anyone what the name of the horse was.'

Before Peterson could answer, Harper had interrupted.

'Sorry! but while I remember, your friend Guthrie thought you might like to know that some retired coastguard called Casson is dead – found shot last night.'

That was a shock, but not as big as the next one.

'The horse,' Peterson said, '2.30 at Doncaster. Been tipped as a good outsider for weeks. I have the occasional bet, you know. The horse's name was Pegasus.' (31)

27

The weather was already bad, and might get worse. I couldn't risk waiting till morning to return to London in case I was late for the meeting with the Prince. Guthrie insisted that I had a light meal before I left. He seemed so upset, I thought that I owed him that.

The weather was getting worse. I was held up for a long time on the Canterbury bypass because of road flooding. It was the early hours of the morning before I got back to my flat in London.

I tried to snatch a few hours' sleep. That was a fatal decision. I woke up late! Peterson lived not far from me. I phoned him to say that there were papers to be collected from my office and delivered to Balfour in Whitehall before he left for Cherton.

Peterson was having car trouble and there weren't many taxis around at that time of morning. My car was outside my apartment. I told Peterson to walk round, collect my keys and take the car. I would get a taxi when I was dressed and breakfasted.

It was eight o'clock when I got to Whitehall. I'd

also arranged for Harper to meet me there so that we could all go together to the Royal Knightsbridge Hotel to pick up the Prince and his party at 9.30.

Balfour had left for Cherton. Harper was there – and so was Peterson – trying to stop the blood which was running from a long cut on his forehead by dabbing it with bits of newspaper.

'Your car is wrapped round a lamp post in St Martin's Lane,' he said. 'Someone had carefully loosened the fluid pipes to your brakes. I've sent for another car for you.'

'Are you all right?' I asked.

'Fine,' he answered, tearing himself off another piece of newspaper. I couldn't help noticing that he was using the racing page.

'You went down to Dover for us, didn't you,' I said. 'I know the story about the 50–1 winner. Can you satisfy my curiosity? Do you know the name of the horse?'

'I can tell you that,' Harper said. 'I won a tenner on it. It was in the 2.30 at Doncaster. The horse's name was Pegasus.' (**31**)

28

I saw that a message was relayed to Cherton to be given to Balfour on his arrival. I'd passed on what description of Pegasus we had and alerted all of our agents at Cherton to widen their search of the area and double-check on everything.

The car that Peterson had ordered for me, to replace my own, had arrived. With it, came a second car for Peterson's own use. The arrangement was for us to drive separately to the Royal Knightsbridge. Harper, then Peterson, would lead the cars to Halfpenny Yard. They would be followed by the Prince. Behind him would be three more cars carrying his own security guards. I would bring up the rear. That way I could keep an eye on the whole procession of vehicles.

The route from the Royal Knightsbridge to Halfpenny Yard had been carefully worked out. Police would be on duty for all of the way and at no time would the vehicles be separated. A helicopter had been assigned to keep a watch on any unusual traffic problems.

The Prince was ready to leave on the minute and the journey was going without any hitch.

Only one thing had slightly surprised me. The car in which the Prince was travelling was a black Rolls Royce – completely bullet proof. The three cars carrying his security guards were all white Mercedes. It had been explained to me that the Rolls was the Prince's own car, shipped from Bohara. The Mercedes were all cars from the Boharan Embassy in London.

I was also worried by the fact that the man driving the middle car of the Mercedes could almost have fitted the description of Pegasus. The Ambassador, who was travelling with the Prince, had assured me that he was a long-standing and trusted member of the security guard of the royal household.

We had now passed Tower Bridge on the south side of the river and were within a little over three miles of Halfpenny Yard. The time was 9.43 – within less than a minute of my time schedule. Everything was going perfectly – and that worried me! However carefully planned, it is never possible, in an operation as complex as this, to forsee every possible problem (**33**).

29

I'd passed Canterbury and joined the M2 Motorway, when I saw a white Mercedes in my driving mirror, coming up behind me, very fast. The road was awash with rain and he was throwing it up like the bow waves of an oncoming ship. I knew he was going to pass too close for comfort. Already on the inside lane, I swerved towards the hard shoulder. In the next instant, my car was drenched in his spray, so that I could see nothing. I guessed that I should be straightening up – but it was too late. I was over the hard shoulder and my two nearside wheels were in a ditch.

By the time I got out of the car, the Mercedes had almost vanished. I was all right. I had one flat tyre, which was in the ditch. That, and the pouring rain, didn't make the job of changing the wheel any easier. By the time I'd done it, I was pretty wet and dirty. I got an old newspaper out of the back of the car to take some of the oil off my hands. It was an evening paper from the day of the Weiler murder. I opened it at the racing page. Not surprisingly, there was only one 50–1 winner – in the 2.30 at Doncaster. The name of the horse was Pegasus.

How could we all have missed it! That Pegasus was running that day could only be coincidence. That the name had been found, perhaps in the cabin where Weiler had been drugged, had to be something else!

'Pegasus' was the code name of an international assassin – probably responsible for a dozen killings of top statesmen in the last ten years. Only two people might have seen him. Both described him as tall, slim, dark-haired and dark-skinned and between thirty and forty. One of those two people was Klaus Weiler. The other was Sir James Knott Balfour, head of Section 6, on his way to Cherton and a meeting of heads of state. Balfour had to be warned!

It was after 7.30. Balfour would have left with the Minister – who had no car radio. I could contact Harper and get him to warn Cherton. Would that be soon enough? Harper *could* take over at Halfpenny Yard. Should I try to catch up on Balfour (**35**), or stick with the Eye of Heaven operation (**34**)?

30

By the time I'd cleared up a few things at the office and collected the cat, it was early evening before I set off for Babworth. I got caught up in the heavy traffic leaving London and it took more than two hours to make the journey. The weather had also broken and it was going to be a dark, wet night.

When I reached Guthrie's cottage, Mrs Waters, his housekeeper, was waiting for me. Guthrie had gone up to Casson's house on the Point. Apparently Casson had been coming down to play chequers. He hadn't arrived and wasn't answering his telephone.

Mrs Waters was obviously waiting to leave. I told her to go and said I would go on up to the Point. It was pouring with rain and I gave her a lift part of the way.

I found Casson's house with all the lights on and the front door open. I called Guthrie's name and got an answer from the kitchen. Casson was lying face up on the kitchen floor with a bullet hole through his forehead. Guthrie was waiting for the local police to arrive. Nothing could be touched, but everything pointed to Casson having been in the middle of packing up to leave when someone had just walked in and shot him.

The police arrived, Guthrie made a brief statement, and I drove him back to the cottage. He was obviously upset and didn't have much to say on the way.

He had a stiff drink and pulled himself together sufficiently to remind me that I had come for a purpose and that we had a job to do. I'd left the cat in a plastic sack in the back of the car and went out to get it. The cat was gone!

Nothing that evening was making much sense. Why would Casson suddenly decide to leave? Who would want to kill him? Why would anyone steal a dead cat – unless it was to prevent my finding out what had killed it.

The rain was still coming down. Though I knew that I should be getting back to London (**27**), Guthrie was pressing me to stay and set off early in the morning (**32**). It was the first time that I'd seen Guthrie nervous and upset.

31

Neither Harper nor Peterson understood the possible significance of what I'd just been told. 'Pegasus' wasn't just a horse – neither the winged creature of Greek mythology nor a 50–1 outsider at Doncaster Races. Pegasus was also the code name of one of Europe's most successful and elusive professional assassins. The name had been linked in recent years with the killings of more than a dozen top statesmen from Paris to Cairo. Pegasus had never been caught. But there was something else, something I knew I should be remembering.

There was a computer terminal in Balfour's office. I tapped in my personal code to give me access to central criminal records. I asked for the file on Pegasus. There was a lot of it. Page after page was flashed up on the screen. Then I saw it! I held the information.

```
DESCRIPTION — UNCERTAIN. PROBABLY MALE.
MAY BE TALL, SLIM, DARK SKINNED, CLEAN
SHAVEN.
AGE COULD BE BETWEEN THIRTY AND FORTY.
ONLY TWO POSSIBLE SIGHTINGS REPORTED.
MAY 1978: INSPECTOR KLAUS WEILER,
DEPARTMENT K, BONN POLICE.
OCTOBER 1981: SIR JAMES KNOTT BALFOUR.
HEAD OF SECTION 6. LONDON METROPOLITAN
POLICE.
```

The pieces were falling into place. Pegasus and Weiler had, perhaps, recognised each other on the Channel ferry. Weiler had to be killed, but he'd left one clue – a clue we'd all missed – the name of a horse on a racing page left on the ferry. Was Pegasus on his way to Cherton? Pegasus might still believe that I was in charge of the Cherton operation – and hence someone's desire to get me out of the way. But now it was Balfour – Balfour, the only other man who might recognise Pegasus! Balfour had to be warned!

'If you're thinking about Balfour's car radio,' Peterson said, 'he hasn't got one. He's gone in the Minister's car. We can get a message to Cherton.'

Would that be soon enough? I had a fast car and might still overtake them. Harper could take over at Halfpenny Yard – though I was still worried about the cat and Mrs McGee's 'funny lights'. Should I go after Balfour (**35**), or stick with the Eye of Heaven (**28**)?

32

Even if the weather didn't improve, it would be daylight by four thirty or five in the morning, making driving that much easier. The Prince and his party weren't due to leave the Royal Knightsbridge Hotel until 9.30, though I wanted to meet Harper and Peterson at Balfour's office in Whitehall at about eight o'clock. If I left Babworth at six, I would have plenty of time to make the journey. I phoned my office to say I was staying in Babworth for the night.

Guthrie's housekeeper had left more than enough food for two, but neither of us felt like eating. Guthrie certainly wasn't his usual talkative self and I began to think that he had something on his mind that he was hesitating to tell me.

It didn't come out until I actually got up to go to my own cottage for some sleep.

'I know it's like speaking ill of the dead,' Guthrie murmured, 'but something has felt wrong ever since that Sunday afternoon we went to see Casson.'

He knew he couldn't leave it there.

'Casson knew the sea around this coast as well as any man, but was he that good? The time the body had been in the water, almost the exact time and place it had entered it . . .'

Guthrie already knew about Weiler.

'There's something else. I had another look at Casson's charts. If the body floated the way he said it did, then it passed over the "Hog's Back" – rocks just below the water's surface that can tear the bottom out of a ship. Yet there was neither a bruise not a cut on the body. I still can't believe it, but if I hadn't known Nick Casson, I'd have said he was in on a "set up" of some sort.'

Guthrie said no more, but I knew what else he was not saying. If Casson was part of a 'set up', and had got nervous about it – nervous enough to pack up and get out – that could be a reason for getting rid of him.

I was still thinking about it when I left Babworth at a little after six next morning, still in pouring rain (**29**).

33

We were now travelling east along London Bridge Road, right on the riverside. Our speed had dropped because we had got behind a small fleet of four or five container lorries which were almost certainly heading for Shuter's Wharf, half a mile ahead of us. There was no point in attempting to overtake them. At any moment, we would be turning off to cross onto the south side of the railway.

Shuter's Wharf was actually the quickest way of reaching Halfpenny Yard, but that was one of the reasons that I hadn't chosen it. I didn't really think there was much danger of an 'ambush', but I'd deliberately avoided using the obvious routes to the Yard. Shuter's Wharf was certainly a place to be avoided. Packed with lorries and stacked crates and with cranes unloading freighters, not only could a small army have been hidden there, but the river offered a perfect means of escape.

My guess had been right. The lorries were going straight on and I could now see Harper, in the leading car, turning off onto Cutler's Bridge over the railway. He would then follow Tower

Road and Dover Way, turning back across the rail-way at New Bridge Road. That way, we would approach the Yard by way of Shoe Lane and Dock Street.

I watched each car as it swung right onto the Bridge. Everyone was still in their place. Travel-ling, as I was, at the rear, I wouldn't see all the cars again until we had crossed Cutler's Bridge and reached the big, Tower Road roundabout on the other side. Because of the curve in the road, there would be several seconds during which I could see little more than the Mercedes in front of me.

As we approached the roundabout they came back into sight – Harper, Peterson, the Prince, the first of the Mercedes . . . The second Mercedes was missing!

There was only one way that the car could have vanished. Instead of going on round the round-about, he must have turned into Vaine Row – and that was the way to Cooper Street! More than ever, I wished that I'd got the answer on that cat! Should I stick with the convoy (**41**), or follow the missing Mercedes (**38**)?

34

I had fondly imagined that, having changed the wheel of my car, I would be able to drive it out of the ditch. I hadn't reckoned on the ground being quite so soft and muddy.

Several passing motorists pulled up on the hard shoulder and a group of four or five of them tried some hard pushing. That did no good. Someone with a big Jaguar got out a tow rope and tried that. It ended with the rope snapping and my car still in the ditch.

I thanked everyone for their efforts and got through to my office on the radio. They contacted the local police who, in turn, called out a local breakdown truck. It was half an hour in arriving.

By the time I was back on the road, it was 8.30. It was pretty certain that I was not going to make the Royal Knightsbridge to pick up the Prince's party at 9.30. Halfpenny Yard was nearer and that still looked possible. Harper was at Balfour's office in Whitehall. I got my office to patch me through to him on the radio and told Harper to take over the operation. I would make straight for Halfpenny Yard.

As I got closer to London, the morning traffic was steadily building up. There was nothing that I could do about it, except keep going. At last, I turned into Dover Way. I looked at my watch. It was 9.40. The Prince would already be on his way to the Yard, but that still gave me twenty minutes to the opening of the time lock on the vault and the beginning of the ceremony.

I was looking for New Bridge Road, the turn off that would take me over the railway, down to the Thames and along Dock Street to Halfpenny Yard. I suddenly realised that the car in front of me was a white Mercedes. I felt certain that it was the same white Mercedes which had forced me off the motorway into the ditch. Certainly, both cars were carrying CD plates. I was close enough to see something of the driver. He was slim, dark-haired, dark-skinned and aged about forty. He looked as if he'd spotted me in his mirror. With hardly room to spare, he pulled out and overtook a wide-bodied truck which was now in front of me (**36**).

35

I made much better time through the London traffic than I expected. Once I got west of the City, the heavy traffic was moving into London and I had a clear road. I knew that Balfour, in the Minister's car, would be taking the M40 motorway to Oxford on the way to Cherton. I was relying on their driver not doing the 135 miles an hour that I was!

I suddenly spotted a white Mercedes in front of me. It had shot in at the last junction and I was almost on top of it! I could see the driver – slim, dark-haired and dark-skinned, aged about forty. I was sure he had seen me. He managed to keep ahead of me, almost as if I were being invited to give chase.

I'd had little time to think about that when I heard the siren of a police car coming up behind me.

With three cars all chasing each other at speeds around 130 miles an hour, it was a situation inviting a bad accident. Silently cursing, I slowed down to let the police catch up with me. The Mercedes was rapidly vanishing into the distance.

I showed my identity to the police and gave a

quick explanation of what was going on. The police were full of apologies until one of the officers in the patrol car suggested that we might not have lost the Mercedes entirely. He'd just been talking on the radio to another motorway patrol, ten miles off and heading towards us down the other carriageway. He got back on the car radio.

No Mercedes had passed them! We looked at the map. There was only one spot he could have left the motorway – by a road which would take him back to London. I'd been fooled!

I turned my car around, taking out six feet of flowering hibiscus which lined the central reservation. At 9.40, I was turning into London Bridge Road, not much more than two miles from Halfpenny Yard and still with twenty minutes to go to the ceremony.

I pulled out from behind a string of heavy trucks and there, in front of me was the Mercedes! Again I was sure that he'd seen me. The odd thing was that he didn't seem to be making any effort to lose me (**39**).

36

I was so interested in the Mercedes that I almost missed New Bridge Road. I caught the street sign out of the corner of my eye, but not before it was too late to make the turn off.

For the moment, I'd lost sight of the Mercedes – though one thing was certain – he hadn't made the turn off either. That didn't put an end to my worries about where he was heading. There were other ways of reaching Halfpenny Yard. If he took the next bridge across the railway, he could cut back towards the Yard by way of Shuter's Wharf. I had to get past that truck in front of me!

Twice, I eased the nose of the car out towards the centre of the road, only to be met with angry screeching of horns from vehicles coming in the other direction. At the third attempt I saw a big enough gap in the oncoming traffic to take a chance. I caught a snatch of something unrepeatable from the open window of a London taxi as I forced the driver to swerve towards the opposite pavement.

I was in front of the truck. The road in front of me was clear. A few hundred yards ahead was the big, Tower Road roundabout. The Mercedes had vanished.

That was no miracle. He need only have crossed the roundabout and he would be out of sight as the road curved sharply towards Cutler's Bridge.

I looked at my watch. It was 9.43. I was still guessing that when he'd crossed Cutler's Bridge he would turn back to Halfpenny Yard by way of the Wharf. If the man in the car was 'Pegasus' and his target was Prince Ali, then his timing was perfect. The buildings would have already been searched. He had only to park the car out of sight and take up a position in a spot overlooking the Yard.

I was almost at the roundabout when another thought struck me. If the Mercedes had not crossed the roundabout, but had swung right into Vaine Row, then he would be on his way to Cooper Street!

The idea of a gunman with a laser rifle still worried me. More than ever, I wished I'd got the answer about that cat! I had to make the decision now. Should I go on over the bridge (**40**), or turn off towards Cooper Street (**38**)?

37

The plan very nearly worked! But for the Boharan Ambassador's chance remark, I could well have missed the bomb in the anteroom – neatly concealed in what should have been a red light bulb and detonated at the perfect moment by the time lock itself!

There were still two questions. 'Who was the real assassin and who was his employer?' My guess was that the assassin was one of the Prince's own security guards and that his employer was Hassan, the Prince's own brother. But I could prove none of it!

It was five weeks later that Balfour sent for me. It was first to tell me a piece of news that hadn't reached me and seemed to have been kept remarkably quiet. A week previously, Prince Hassan had been 'accidentally' drowned while bathing in one of the royal swimming pools. It was a piece of news which had encouraged Balfour to authorise a bit of 'digging' in the ruins of Victoria House!

'If you're going to assassinate someone,' Balfour said, 'and you could make it look like something else – like a jewel theft – why would you pass up the chance?'

He threw something blue and shiny across the desk. 'Not the Eye of Heaven – a good glass copy. Part of the vaults at Victoria House survived the collapse of the building. That was brought up in its package from the ruins. I've also done another piece of 'digging' – on our friend Colby. He wasn't always called Colby. He once worked for Prince Hassan while the Sultan was in exile. He also once worked at Victoria House.'

I had the picture. Colby had stolen the real Eye of Heaven for Hassan. That was why Prince Ali had to be killed before the vault was opened and the fake stone was discovered.

'What do we do now?' I asked.

'Nothing!' was Balfour's answer. 'I'm sorry about Weiler. Hassan's death looks like a piece of rough justice. As to this "Eye of Heaven", we keep it. Bohara is a key State in Middle East politics. If ever we need their co-operation, that might be the time to reveal to Ali that we too have "seen through the Eye of Heaven"!'

38

As I swung the car into Vaine Row, I saw the Mercedes! It was parked near the end of Cooper Street in the small cul-de-sac which ended in the fence of the railway embankment. It looked empty. It would be if its occupant was making his way along the embankment to the backs of 72 and 74 Cooper Street!

I got on the car radio to the office and got them to patch me through direct to the observation post in Tanner's Lane. Bates and Driscoll were on duty.

I told them to arm themselves, leave the post by the quickest route – if they were seen that was just unfortunate – and get to 72 and 74. I didn't care how they got in. I would worry about search warrants later. They were looking for a marksman, probably armed with a laser rifle and who would be positioning himself on the top floor of one of the two houses. He would be at the back. His target was Halfpenny Yard, across the railway. I'd get a back-up unit to them but, with perhaps no more than ten minutes left, it was going to be up to them. I too was on my way.

I stopped my car behind the Mercedes, so that

he couldn't use it to make a getaway. I took my Smith and Wesson from the glove compartment, climbed the fence onto the railway and started to run along the embankment.

I had no difficulty in knowing when I had reached the back of number 74. The back windows were open on both the first and second floors. Through them, I could hear Bates and Mrs McGee having a verbal 'set-to'. Driscoll opened the window of the top floor of 72 and did her best to make herself heard. There was a way through from the top floor of 74 into 72. Somebody had been up there, but both houses were empty of any gunman. I knew I'd been fooled.

It was 9.55. The Prince and his party would already be in the Victoria House vault. In five minutes, the time lock would open.

I started to run across the railway lines. I lost more than a minute waiting for a slow goods train to pass by. I was at the embankment on the opposite side, over the fence and running through the rubble of the part-demolished building at the end of the Yard. My watch showed twenty-five seconds to ten (**45**).

39

I was now right on the tail of the Mercedes. We were travelling quite fast with the road, just for the moment, fairly free of traffic in our direction, though a solid stream was coming the other way.

We were now getting near the end of London Bridge Road. If we went straight on, we would be onto Shuter's Wharf. Less than a quarter mile from the farther end of the Wharf, was Halfpenny Yard.

If the man driving the car in front of me was, in fact, 'Pegasus', and his target was Prince Ali, he must know who I was. Why then, did he seem to be happy to have me sitting on his tail?

That last question was answered only a few seconds later. We were approaching the last turn off before Shuter's Wharf – the road which crossed Cutler's Bridge onto the other side of the railway. Without a signal, or any kind of warning, the Mercedes suddenly swung out, passed between two trucks coming in the opposite direction, by nothing more than a hair's breadth, and was off towards the bridge.

Totally unprepared for what had happened, I had already passed the turning. Traffic was now coming up behind me. I couldn't back and I could see nowhere in front of me where I could turn round. I knew that I'd lost the Mercedes!

I stopped the car and looked at the time. It was 9.43. On the other side of Cutler's Bridge was the Tower Road roundabout. There were only two ways off it. If the Mercedes went straight on, then within another three quarters of a mile, he could turn back over the railway and reach Halfpenny Yard from the other side. If he turned left at the roundabout, that would bring him into Vaine Row – and that was the way to Cooper Street!

Cooper Street still worried me. It was a perfect position for a gunman with a high-powered laser rifle. It might have been easier if I'd got the answer about that cat! I'd used three more minutes just weighing the possibilities and there was no time for me to try both places.

If the man had gone to Halfpenny Yard, then my quickest way there was to drive straight on across Shuter's Wharf (**40**). If it was Cooper Street, I had to turn round somewhere and get over the bridge (**38**).

40

It was now 9.49. The Prince and his party would be arriving at the Yard at any second. If the Mercedes was parked, I didn't expect it to be where I could see it – and there was no time to search for it. I'd crossed the Wharf. Now there was only Hanby Street, then the Yard itself.

As I passed the end of Hanby Street I caught a flash of white. I braked hard. Just visible at the far end of the street where it opened out into a small square was the white tail-end of a car! It had to be the Mercedes!

There were only two ways out of Hanby Street to the Yard. The one by the railway was too open. He must have gone through the half-demolished building almost opposite Victoria House. I took my Smith and Wesson from the glove compartment, jumped out of the car, and started to run.

The man was exactly where I expected him to be – at the end of the ruined building, facing towards Victoria House. I shouted. He whipped round, taking two quick shots at me with a hand gun. Before I could return fire, the man was over a wall and into the Yard. He hadn't counted on the two marksmen I'd stationed on the rooftops. I heard two rifle shots but when I reached the Yard, it was empty!

'He's slipped into Victoria House!' came a shout from above me. Before I could answer, the leading car of the Prince's party turned into the Yard. I signalled it to stop.

Harper joined me. I told him that our man had run into the building. Harper was ready to go in after him. I shook my head. The man was soon going to find that there was no way out – except the way he'd gone in. He was trapped, and I was prepared to wait. Harper went back to tell the Prince.

Not much more than five minutes later a gun was thrown out of the door of Victoria House and a man appeared with his hands on his head. I beckoned him to come forward.

He was still fifty yards off when he looked as if he might be going to drop one of his hands. One of my marksmen reacted a little too quickly. There was only one shot. The man in front of me literally exploded (**42**)!

41

I got on the car radio to my office and told them to patch me through to the observation post in Tanner's Lane. Bates and Driscoll were on duty. I told them to forget the observation, arm themselves and, any way they had to, get up to the top floors of numbers 72 and 74 Cooper Street. They could be looking for a marksman armed with a laser rifle. There was no time to get them any back-up. They were on their own.

We had reached the Yard. I drove my car down the pavement, just past the Prince's Rolls, to give him that much extra cover for his walk to the door of Victoria House.

I breathed more easily once we were all in the anteroom outside the vaults and waiting only for the time lock to release. Everything and everyone – including the Prince – had been thoroughly searched, and I could see no way that any weapon or explosive device could have been hidden. I was still uneasy.

The clock on the wall showed 9.55. The Ambassador was explaining to the Prince that when it reached ten o'clock, the red light would come on over the door to show that the time lock had released. The normal combination lock could then be operated.

I'd left Peterson outside standing by the car radio for news of Bates and Driscoll in Cooper Street. We still had to get the Prince, and the Eye of Heaven, safely back into his car.

I had time to go outside to check with Peterson. Even when the time lock released, it could take two or three minutes to deal with the combination lock and swing open the heavy door. Harper could do both of those things.

As I moved towards the stairs out of the anteroom I got a sudden prickling sensation in the nape of my neck. Twice before in my life I'd got that feeling. Twice before it had been an odd warning of danger! Could I have missed something – something which might threaten my life, or those I was about to leave behind in the anteroom?

Should I go to see Peterson (**45**), or should I clear everyone out of the building – for no reason I could explain, and knowing that the greatest danger to the Prince might still lie in those last few yards to reach his car (**43**)?

42

The blast threw me to the ground. I picked myself up to see nothing but still burning fragments scattering the ground.

No-one was going into those vaults until I'd had the bomb squad through them with a fine-tooth comb. I spoke to the Prince. He understood the situation and, to my relief, proposed an indefinite postponement of the ceremony.

The Prince returned to Bohara that day and my investigations began. The man was unidentifiable, even from what fragments remained of his teeth. The car in Hanby Street was identified as one reported stolen from the Boharan Embassy two weeks before. It held no clues.

The vaults in Victoria House were undamaged and, when the time lock opened at 10.00, the Eye of Heaven was still in its place. The only curious fact which emerged when Selby and Mayhew, the makers, checked the door and time lock, was that the light bulb which signalled the opening of the door, was missing. They admitted one of their own men could have taken it hoping to find a better match to the original.

Nothing unusual happened at Cherton, much to Balfour's relief, and the heads of state returned safely to their own countries.

The killing of Nick Casson remains an unsolved and apparently motiveless crime. There were no more attempts upon my life and I could only assume that they were connected with the intention to assassinate the Prince.

Balfour was prepared to accept that the man shot and blown to pieces in Halfpenny Yard was 'Pegasus'. I was never so sure, particularly when a report from Buenos Aires, from a usually reliable source, suggested that 'Pegasus' had been killed in South America twelve months before.

Three months after the Prince's visit came news that his brother, Hassan, had been killed in a plane crash. Ali was now ruler of Bohara. The Eye of Heaven was to be handed to the Boharan Ambassador, still in its sealed package. It would be returned to Bohara by special messenger. I never saw the Eye of Heaven, but I was sure it was not the only part of this mystery which I had failed to see.

43

I'd opened my mouth to give the order to evacuate the building when, what had been no more than a 'feeling' of danger became a reality! The words of the Boharan Ambassador had suddenly flashed through my mind: 'When the red light comes on over the door . . .' I was looking at the light over the door. It *was* red – and the last time I'd seen it, it had been white!

'Everybody out!' I shouted. 'Don't panic – but move quickly out of the building and into the Yard outside.'

I led the Prince myself while Harper shepherded the others. We had reached the street door when the explosion occurred. Smoke was rolling up the stairs from the vault and beginning to fill the corridor behind us. As everyone ran out into the Yard, there was a second loud sound, not an explosion, but a slow rumbling. I looked up in time to see a crack zig-zag up the face of the building!

'Get away from the building and the cars!' I shouted. 'Make for the other side of the Yard. The whole building is going to come down!'

We all stood at a safe distance, watching the

walls of Victoria House sinking down through a cloud of smoke and dust to become no more than a pile of rubble. I turned to the Prince.

'I'm afraid,' he said, in quiet, faultless English, 'that the ceremony will have to be delayed – perhaps indefinitely. But please don't apologise. I owe you my life, and something else which you may not understand. There is a saying in my country, "Fear him who can see through the eye of Heaven, for from him, there is nothing hidden".'

The Prince flew back to Bohara on the following day and my investigations began. The first clue really came from Babworth, the place where it had all begun. Guthrie was now convinced that Weiler's body could not have floated from the ferry to Babworth beach without some visible damage to the skin, and that Casson could not have pinpointed so well exactly when and where it had entered the water. He was sure that Weiler had never been on the ferry. The body had been kept in sea water for four days, then brought to the beach, probably by a small boat (**44**).

44

In case it should be missed, or even washed out to sea again, somebody had to be paid to 'find' it. Casson was ideal. His knowledge and experience were enough to convince even Guthrie and myself that it could have come from one of the cross-Channel ferries. Casson was a basically honest man. Having taken the money, he had got cold feet and attempted to run. He had to be eliminated. That was the only explanation of an otherwise motiveless murder and the appearance in Casson's normally modest bank account of a cash deposit of £5,000!

The whole scheme was intended to suggest that Pegasus, a known international assassin, was on his way to the heads of state meeting at Cherton. Weiler could recognise Pegasus. That was why Weiler was chosen to be killed. Any attempt on my life was because it was believed that I was still in charge of the Cherton operation.

It was also meant that the ferry steward, Colby, was in on the scheme, though that would be difficult to prove. He had to tell a story which would appear to confirm that both Pegasus and Weiler were on the ferry. The fact that a horse called 'Pegasus' was running on that very day, had to have been no more than a piece of luck. It provided the perfect 'clue' – or it would have if Colby hadn't slipped up by not telling anyone the name of the horse!

Cooper Street really had no connection with the plan. What Mrs McGee had heard upstairs, was Roper, who was eventually recaptured in Leeds. The 'funny lights' turned out to be no more than a form of 'spots before the eyes'. Mrs McGee suffered from high blood pressure. The body of the cat was never found, but while one of my officers was making enquiries in the Cooper Street area, she accidently heard exactly how the cat had been killed. It had been struck by a car in Vaine Row, and the poor beast had then crawled as far as the car breaker's yard before it died.

The story of the cat was not yet over. The real victim of the intended assassination had always been Prince Ali. When it looked as though the clues about Cherton had failed, the cat's body was stolen to suggest that if there was a threat to the Prince, it lay in Cooper Street (**37**).

45

Apart from the marksmen who I knew were stationed on the roofs, the Yard looked empty, but for the line of cars and Peterson standing by one of them, directly outside Victoria House. I looked again at my watch. It was two seconds off ten o'clock.

I opened my mouth to speak to Peterson when the explosion occurred. We could feel it, rather than see it, but there was no doubt it had come from the vaults. Within seconds, the corridor within the doorway had filled with billowing smoke which was drifting out into the Yard.

From the smoke, his hands and face blackened, still beating flames from his clothes, staggered Harper.

'I was just by the door of the anteroom!' he gasped. 'They've all got to be dead in there!'

Peterson saw to Harper while I used a car radio to call up fire and ambulance.

The firemen got through the smoke with breathing apparatus. Harper had been right. Prince Ali and all the others in the anteroom were dead.

The safe door was jammed by the explosion, but the vaults were still standing. There were the expected diplomatic protests from Bohara about our failure to protect the Prince's life. Some weeks later, when the vaults had been repaired, we received instructions that the Eye of Heaven, still safe in its sealed package, was to be handed over to the Boharan Ambassador for return to his country by special messenger.

Casson's murder remains a motiveless and unsolved crime. If Pegasus did cross to this country his target does not seem to have been at Cherton. It could have been Prince Ali, but I believed that that killing had been arranged by one of his own security guards in the pay of his brother, Hassan.

Somebody had been using the top floor of 74 Cooper Street, but it was probably Roper. He was later rearrested in Birmingham.

I had a lot of theories, but very little evidence to prove any of them. I was sorry for Weiler, Casson and Prince Ali. I was sure that, in some way, their deaths were all connected with the Eye of Heaven. I had never even seen the stone, but wondered whether 'Heaven' would approve of its title.

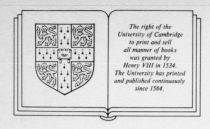

Published by the Press Syndicate of the University of Cambridge
The Pitt Building, Trumpington Street, Cambridge CB2 1RP
32 East 57th Street, New York, NY 10022, USA
10 Stamford Road, Oakleigh, Melbourne 3166, Australia

First published 1985

Printed in Great Britain by the Guernsey Press Co. Ltd, Guernsey

Library of Congress catalogue card number: 84–19951

British Library cataloguing in publication data
Sharp, Allen
The Eye of Heaven – (Storytrails)
I. Title   II. Series
823′.914[J]   PZ7
ISBN 0 521 31707 X

Map by Celia Hart
Cover illustration by Robin Lawrie

DS